WOGGALIZARDS

These imaginary lizards only exist in West Woggle.

T. REX

The T. rex had the biggest teeth of any of the dinosaurs — they were sharp as blades and grew to be nine inches long.

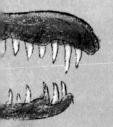

 ## ROCK

Rocks have been around a long time. They make good starter pets.

The OodleThunks

Welcome to Camp Woggle

THE OODLETHUNKS

Welcome to Camp Woggle

ADELE GRIFFIN
ART BY **MIKE WU**

SCHOLASTIC PRESS
NEW YORK

Text copyright © 2017 by Adele Griffin
Illustrations copyright © 2017 by Mike Wu

Library of Congress Cataloging-in-Publication Data available

ISBN 978-0-545-73291-8

10 9 8 7 6 5 4 3 2 1   17 18 19 20 21

Printed in the U.S.A.   23
First edition, August 2017

Book design by Phil Falco

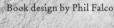

For Hace, my Bonk.
A.G.

For "Goo Jai," my Granny Thunk.
M.W.

NORTH GLOGGLE
WEST WOGGLE
Rattletrap Bridge
Eggy
Wilderness
Hatching Meadow
Little Peat School Cave
Dragknuckle Bridge
Gurds' Cave
No-Name River
Mauro's Cave
Mt. URP
Old Brou's Cave
Rock Park

MEET THE OODLETHUNKS!

SCHOOL'S OUT

"Woooooo-hoooooooooo!" I yelled. That was my official sound of summer!

"Woooooo-heeeeeeee!" yelled my little brother, Bonk, who liked to copy me.

"Hooooooooo-weeeeeeee!" yelled everyone as we came tearing out of Little Peat School Cave.

Miss Moony, Master Og, and Miss Gog waved us good-bye. "Have a fun summer, kiddos!" They looked happy, too. We *all* needed a break from school—and that's what summer vacation was about.

Our stegosaurus, Stacy Steg Oodlethunk, was waiting for Bonk and me in the schoolyard.

"Yeeeee-hawwwww!" we yelled as we jumped

1

all over Stacy, rubbing her chin and behind her ears as she *urrrrmp*ed with joy.

We were the only kids in West Woggle who had a dinosaur for a pet. Luckily for everyone, we were good sharers. Most kids had smaller pets like Storm, the fruitafossor of my best friend, Erma. And just last week, Erma's little sister, Iggy, got a baby fruitafossor that she named Rain.

Bruce Brute had a goat.

Ezra Droog took care of a family of lizards.

Meadow Stalagmite owned a rock named Keith. (She said she was not ready for an alive pet.)

All the way down and around Mount Urp, we played our favorite game, clonk-bonk-you're-it. Our last game of the school year.

"Everyone is jealous that we get to ride home on Stacy, while they have to walk," said Bonk once the setting sun meant it was time to head home.

"True," I agreed. "But then we have to spend time foraging for Stace's dinner."

"Ugh!" said Bonk. "That's also true."

Stacy was part pet but also part wild. Her small mouth worked hard to fill her enormous body. She spent her day rooting for grass and moss. Bonk and I helped. Tonight we gathered armfuls of liverworts, plus we sneaked her some of our own dinner—pine-nut pudding and honey-baked carrots.

"Kids, tonight's an Oodle-*think* dinner," announced Mom, scratching her head with both hands. "So use your Neander-noggins. Now that school is done, who do you want to help out this summer? Dad or me?"

"DAD!" we both shouted.

"Oh." Mom drooped. "Guess there wasn't much to think about after all."

"Sorry, Mom," I said. "It's a no-brainer."

During summer break, West Woggle kids worked for their parents. The top ten grown-up jobs in West Woggle were:

1. hunter
2. gatherer
3. chiseler
4. teacher
5. potter
6. tall-tale teller
7. painter
8. gardener
9. volcano watcher

Mom worked in the tenth-most popular job—advertising.

Luckily, Dad was a gatherer. Unlike Mom, he

spent his days in the great outdoors, where he looked for delicious new Wogglian foods.

"Okay, Oodlethunkies. Early to bed. We want to be up with the sun," said Dad.

"Can Stacy gather with us tomorrow?" I asked. "She liked following us to school all spring. It gave her something to do."

"Sorry, Oona," said Dad. "You know how much I love Stace, but that steg eats more than she gathers. She should stay home in the yard."

Not good. Stacy needed to keep busy. If we were gone all day, she might get into mischief.

The next morning, and the next and the next, Bonk and I were up with Dad to gather in the fields of West Woggle. We discovered boysenberry patches, a new kind of wild green onion, some species of mushrooms that made us all really sick, and one species of mushroom that did not.

In the yard at home, Stacy was also hard at work.

One day, she unbuilt our rock wall.

The next day, she ate the tops of Mom's prized swampweed trees.

And the day after that, she dug herself a huge mud bath.

"This can't go on," said Mom. "Stacy is becoming a cave wrecker."

"She's bored and lonely," I explained.

"Leave her some toys to play with," said Dad.

But Stacy had outgrown her walnut doll and her painted stones. She didn't mean to ruin our home. She only wanted to keep busy.

The next day, while we were up near Listening Hill gathering sunflowers, we ran into the Gurds looking for elephant-ear plants.

"Storm chewed a hole in Mom's latest

invention," said Erma. "See? It's called an umbrella, and it's for keeping the rain off."

I inspected the umbrella. I could see how it might have kept the rain off. But that hole in the middle was an issue. "Stacy also messes up stuff while we are out and about," I said.

Iggy sighed. "Our pets cause trouble when we're gone. But what can we do?"

It was a problem, and I didn't know how to solve it.

Coming home, we saw our neighbor, Bruce Brute, tying up his pet goat, Baa.

Usually I tried to avoid smelly, gross Bruce, but this afternoon he looked sad.

"What's wrong, Bruce?" I asked.

"Baa Brute is not allowed in our cave anymore," said Bruce. "I'm out all day helping my folks with the dairy. When I get home, Baa is too excited to see me. So he kicks and butts his head and chews the rug."

"Our pets are going crazy this summer!" cried Bonk. "Woggle needs help."

"Too bad our whole collection of animals can't meet up and play," said Bruce.

The idea went through me like a *thud*. Like that time I was sitting under an avocado tree and an avocado dropped on my head.

"Collected Animals Meeting Place!" I shouted. "Let's do it! Let's give our pets what they need most this summer!"

"What's that?" asked Bonk and Bruce together.

"CAMP, of course!" I answered.

CAMP!

NOT THAT KIND OF PET

Dad and Mom agreed to my Collected Animals Meeting Place at once.

"We need to help Stacy more than you need to help Dad," said Mom. "Camp sounds like a smart invention. Tonight, you can explain the rules."

"Yes! Sound the Watch Drum and make a speech," said Dad. "Then sign 'em up."

Tonight was West Woggle's Wild Rumpus. It was the longest day of the year. To celebrate, all the local families got together on Slabtop Mountain for a huge potluck dinner. *Pot* meant each family brought a large pot of food. The *luck* part was that you could eat whatever you wanted and ignore any pots of weird glop.

Bonk wanted in on my great camp idea—who wouldn't? Quickly, he and I chiseled out the CAMP RULES tablet to bring up to Slabtop.

"These are good rules," said Bonk when we were done. "But we might get a lot of questions. What do we do when we don't know the answer?"

"Always answer YES," I told him. "That is a way more fun answer than NO."

We helped Dad prepare a stack of hazelnut pancakes with teenyberry jam for the potluck. We also made him leave his snail-on-a-stick

treats at home. Dad sometimes got too creative with his Oodlethunk Delights foods.

Finally, we jumped on Stacy and headed out. "Ah! What a luxury, to travel by stegomotion," said Mom, rubbing her feet as she leaned against Stacy's back plates. "Especially when I've been in these bone-heeled shoes."

Stacy was happy to give us a lift. She'd been cooped up in the yard all day, and she'd chewed her pillow to pieces.

Slabtop Mountain was packed. Erma and Iggy, plus their mom and their two fruitafossors, Storm and Rain, already had selected a nice smooth spot. We parked next to them, and then we headed to the buffet.

Sadly, they were almost out of salted-cricket crisps. But there was still plenty of food left: dandelion soup, spicy bristlecone salad, cold roasted artichokes, triple-berry smash, and something new called chickpea pie.

Chickpea pie? Cutest pie name ever! And it smelled good, too.

I scooped out my first helping and then my second helping, so that I wouldn't need to make an extra trip.

On the way back to our pelt, Erma and I ran into a kid I'd never seen before. "Oona, this is Mauro Ongeri," said Erma. "He's my new neighbor. His family has moved here from South Gloggle."

"Hi," said Mauro.

"Hi," I said. "I'm Oona Oodlethunk. Do you have a pet?"

"Yes," said Mauro. "But he's napping. He might come by later."

"You don't keep him tied up?"

Mauro laughed. "Nah. Inglebert can chew through anything."

"No matter *what* pet you've got, you are very lucky to meet me," I said. "My brother and I are starting a camp for pets. We're giving a speech about it after dinner."

"Cool," said Mauro. He looked in my food bowl. "And you are very lucky to meet me. My family brought the chickpea pie. Is this camp of yours for *all* pets?"

"Yes," I said. "Is Inglebert a lizard?" Mauro looked like a lizard guy.

"Not really . . ." Mauro shrugged. "My pet is more like a reptile."

"We welcome all shapes and sizes of animals at our camp," I assured him.

"Great," said Mauro. "Can't wait to hear more. Enjoy your chickpeas."

I did. I ate my first and second helpings. Once everyone had finished their potluck and

finished all their burps and teeth picking, Bonk
and I gave each other the signal.

Bonk sounded the West Woggle drum for
quiet.

The picnickers hushed.

We jumped to the front of the picnic area so
that everybody saw us.

"WOGGLIANS!" I bellowed. "MY
BROTHER AND I ARE STARTING A COL-
LECTED ANIMALS MEETING PLACE!"

"IT'S CALLED CAMP, AND IT WILL BE FUN!" yelled Bonk.

That was the end of our speech.

"Any questions?" I asked.

There was a waving of clubs as we took questions from the crowd.

"Do you do early drop-off?"

"Will there be games?"

"Will there be crafts?"

"Will there be nap times?"

"Will there be lunch?"

"Can you offer late pickup?"

"YES! YES! YES! YES! YES! YES!" we bellowed.

"My pet is allergic to peanuts," yelled Meadow. "Will he be safe?"

"YES—I did not know that about Keith," I said. "It's a peanut-free camp." Meadow always had interesting information about the pet rocks in her collection.

"My pet goat is smart and gets bored," said Bruce. "Will he learn new things?"

"YES! Your pets will learn lots of useful things," Bonk told him. "Also, goats aren't smart."

I frowned at Bonk. "Your pet will learn friendly competition," I told Bruce. "Plus teamwork and cooperation skills."

"Where should we bring our pet to sign up for camp?" asked Erma.

"Old Tooth Fort!" said Bonk.

Whoa, Bonk! Good quick thinking! I gave him a thumbs-up.

One club had been waving for a long time.

"You, in the back?" I pointed.

The new kid, Mauro, stepped forward. "Inglebert isn't a pet species that you find in Woggle. May I bring him?"

"Mauro, like I said, we welcome *all* pets. As you can see, we have a steg," I said, trying not to sound too braggy. "No pet in Woggle is more unusual than Stacy. And Stacy is *definitely* allowed to go to our camp."

"Pssst! Oona! Maybe we should meet

Inglebert first?" whispered Bonk. He pointed to rule number four on our Camp Rules tablet.

"Actually," said Mauro. "I think I hear him." He set his ear to the ground. "Yup. He's up from his nap and on his way. I will introduce him to everyone."

That's when I noticed something unusual about Slabtop Mountain. Birds and monkeys were chattering extra nervously in the trees. Not good.

"Hey, Mauro. Is your pet a dangerous predator?" I asked.

"Weeeeelll . . . he looks a lot more dangerous than he is," said Mauro.

Somewhere in the distance, a woolly mammoth blew a warning. This sound was followed by the rumble of the whole herd running away.

Then the grasses and trees of Slabtop Mountain went still. As if all the animals were too scared to make noise.

The only sound was *thudda thudda thudda thudda.*

Whatever was coming, it was coming closer. Closer.

We looked to the right. We looked to the left.

We were all trying to figure it out.

"Wogglians, if you would please stay calm, Inglebert is nothing to be scared of." But Mauro was the only one who looked calm.

Everyone else looked petrified.

THUDDA   THUDDA   THUDDA THUDDATHUDDATHUDDA.

Was it . . . ? Could it be . . . ?

Most of us had never seen a real one—except for old Mr. Thagomizer. And he was the first of us who knew for sure.

"Oh no!" he yelped. "Oh no, oh no, OH NO!"

As the beast came racing into sight over the far end of Slabtop Mountain, old Mr. Thagomizer yelped and dove into the nearest horsetail plant.

The rest of us were too stunned to move.

That huge head! Those giant teeth!

And then—FEAR FRENZY! Everybody

began screaming and running in all different directions.

"MOM! DAD! JUMP ON STACY!" yelled Bonk.

"THERE'S NO TIME TO LOSE!" My hand shot out to grab Mom's and swing her up. "INGLEBERT IS . . . IS A . . . IS A . . ." I could barely get the bellow out.

Luckily, every other voice on Slabtop Mountain could help me.

"T. REX!"

CAMP RULES

1. No chewing or biting
   (unless it's your food)

2. Be kind and thoughtful

3. Older pets get first turn

4. No dangerous predators
   allowed

5. When nature calls, wash
   your paws

SHE'S BAAAAAAAACK

Stacy galloped us home faster than I'd ever seen her move.

Poor Dad, who'd been slow and low on the jump, had to bump along while hanging on to Stace by her fear-charged, spike-stiffened tail.

Even though Stacy was the only one running, by the time we returned to our cave-sweet-cave, we were all out of breath. It was warm outside, but Mom built up a fire anyway so that we could feel cozy and safe.

"Wheeee-ew! The *T* in T. rex should stand for *Terrifying*!" exclaimed Dad. "My throat is dry from screaming! Who wants a soothing lemon-and-honey?"

"Me, me, me!" we all shouted.

Stace flopped straight into her mud bath. After the last rain, our front yard puddle had grown into a pond. Now Stacy took a mighty drink.

"Thanks for saving us *again*, Stace," said Bonk as we hugged her. This past winter, Stacy had grown to full height and weight, and by using all her tremendous strength, she had rescued us from an avalanche. She was one special steg.

"How scary to see a real live T. rex in this modern age!" said Mom once we were glugging lemon-and-honeys around the fire.

"He was truly horrible!" Dad made a T. rex shadow on the cave wall, already practicing his tall tale.

"The thing is," said Bonk slowly, "I don't think Inglebert was even a full-grown T. rex."

"Of course he was. He was gigantic," said Mom.

"I agree with Bonk," I said. "I think he was more like a baby."

"Kids, he was full grown," said Dad, "and dangerous!"

"A little baby T.!" argued Bonk and me.

"A terrifying adult T.!" shouted our parents.

"HE WAS AN ITTY-WITTY BABY!" bellowed Bonk and me.

"HE WAS BIGGITY BIG BIG!" roared our parents.

We all jumped to our feet, snarling and beating our clubs.

"OODLETHUNKS!"

The voice was unmistakable. We dropped our clubs and turned to see.

"She's baaaaaack," whispered Mom.

"Egad," Dad whispered back.

"Dave, what does *egad* mean?" whispered Mom.

"I don't know. But it sounded better than *ugh*," whispered Dad.

"End of school always means one other thing," said Bonk.

"It's a thing we forget," I said. "And we forgot this time, too."

Every year, right around now, Granny Grandthunk came to visit.

"Family! Don't just stand there clubbing around!" scolded Granny. She set down her tortoiseshell luggage. "I've walked across Woggle to see you. Bring me my lemon-and-honey!"

"Yes, Mom," said our mom. She went to get Granny a cup.

"Granny Grandthunk! Feels like you were just here," said Dad. "Take the softest pelt and rest your old bones."

"Who are you calling *old*?" Granny grunted. "Oona! Bonk! Front and center! Come let me inspect you!"

We scrambled to be inspected.

"Whoa! I'm waaay taller than you now, Granny," I said.

"Even I'm a little bit taller than you now!" said Bonk.

"Are you calling me *short*?" Granny jumped to her tiptoes.

Just then, Stacy poked her head through the window and gave Granny a slurp.

"You have a face washer? When did things get so fancy around here?" Granny squinted. Besides being old and short, Granny was a bit blind.

"That's not a face washer. That's our newest Oodlethunk," said Dad. "Stacy is a stegosaurus. In fact, she's the only stegosaurus in Woggle."

"Is that right? When I was a girl, I could leg-wrestle any steg in Woggle," said Granny. "You want to know the trick to leg-wrestling a steg? Smart angles, good fakes, and never say 'Uncle!'" She dropped to the ground and rolled over on her back to show us her moves. "Who wants to challenge me? Never hurts to try! I'll go easy on you! If you get pinned, just say 'Uncle!'"

"That's tempting, Mom," said our mom. "But I think you need some rest."

Granny wasn't ready to rest. "Also, you gotta make your face mean as a Dunkleosteus! Ever seen one of those? They have huge, hard eyeballs! How hard can you make your eyeballs, kids? Give it a shot!"

"We're pretty tired," said Mom. "Earlier tonight, we were chased from our potluck by a humongous T. rex."

"Baby T.," I said-coughed into my hand.

Granny looked shocked. "Are dinosaurs making a comeback in Woggle? That's wild! I've never even seen a T. rex!"

"It was incredibly frightening, Granny," said Dad.

"Of course *you* thought so, Dave." Granny

made a face. "I always tell my friends—Dave's got no killer instinct! No hunt in him! No guts!"

"Okay," said Mom. "Time for bed, everybody." She began to beat out the fire.

"Kids, since Granny feels so relaxed around dinosaurs, maybe she could go with you and Stace tomorrow? To help set up camp?" suggested Dad.

Bonk and I gave Dad our hardest eyeballs.

We did NOT want to be in charge of Granny.

"I'm in," said Granny. She speared a wall slug and sucked it between her front teeth. "Good night!" Then she fell back on her pelt, fast asleep.

"Looks like Granny's all yours," whispered Dad over Granny's snoring.

"We're fine with that," I said. "Granny does better with kids and animals."

But I knew the look on Bonk's face echoed what I was thinking: UGH. And also EGAD.

Granny was a lot of work.

Late that night, I woke up to the sounds of

scuffling. I jumped down from my bunk to Bonk's bed. Bonk was awake.

"Do you hear that, too?" he asked. "It's from outside."

We raced to the window.

By the light of the moon, we saw Granny Grandthunk out in the yard. She was leg-wrestling Stacy.

"It's a shame," I said after we'd watched for a while. "Each time Granny thinks she is about to win, Stacy pins her. But you have to admit, Granny's got sass."

"She is also embarrassing," said Bonk.

"But maybe she'll know what to do if Mauro tries to bring his T. rex to camp."

"No way would Mauro bring him. Not after what Inglebert did tonight."

"Inglebert didn't do anything tonight," I said. "He just showed up."

Outside the window, we heard Granny yelp, "Uncle!"

"Anyway, I doubt they'll come," I said.

"Camp Woggle isn't the right place for a T. rex," agreed Bonk.

"Exactly. Good night, Bonk."

"Good night, Oona."

But as we climbed back in our bunks, I knew we both were shivering at the idea of a T. rex at Camp Woggle.

Even an itty-bitty baby one.

FIGHT, FEED, FIGHT

The next morning, our cave looked different.

"Granny, did you rearrange our furniture?" asked Dad.

"Yes! While I was cleaning up. This cave was filthy," said Granny. "I gave it a sunrise scrub. And Stacy got a bath. You're welcome!"

Stacy did look squeaky clean. She also seemed to think that Granny was her new boss.

"Sit!" said Granny. Stacy sat. Granny tossed her a branch of teenyberries.

"Eat!" said Granny. Stacy ate the berries.

When it came time to leave for Old Tooth Fort, Granny clicked her tongue. Stacy kneeled her front legs so Granny could hop on Stacy's back.

When Bonk and I tried to get a lift, too, Granny thwacked her club at us.

"You kids need to walk," said Granny. "Build up those weakling leg muscles. I'm only enjoying a ride because I don't want to wreck my new shoes." She stuck them out to show us.

"Gorgeous! Where did you get those?" asked Mom.

Granny wiggled her eyebrows. "Spoils of war," she said mysteriously. She clicked again, and Stacy started to move at a trot.

"And here I didn't think Stacy could be trained," I told Bonk as we jogged behind our steg's tail, which swooshed back and forth on the forest floor.

"Depends on who's doing the training," shouted Granny from up front.

Old Tooth Fort was at the base of Slabtop Mountain. It was made from the huge teeth of creatures that once had roamed Woggle.

Sometimes Erma's mom used it as a pop-up shop for her newest inventions.

Sometimes the Woggle Scouts used it for their base camp.

Sometimes travelers needed it as a place to rest.

"And now Old Tooth Fort will be our CAMP pet headquarters," I said.

Earlier this morning, Bonk and I had clay-painted a bright sign that read CAMP WOGGLE. Now we hung it from Old Tooth Fort's front tooth.

Next we unpacked two piles of snacks: leaves and moss for the vegetarian pets, and chew bones for the carnivores.

We chiseled out the day's camp activities.

"All that's left to do is wait for the pets to show up," I said.

"What do animals *do* at Camp Woggle anyhow?" asked Granny. "Compete to the death?"

"No way! Pets meet here to make friends and to learn new things," I said.

"Hahahahaha!" Granny pinched a slug off a leaf and swallowed it. "You know what animals like to do? Fight, feed, and fight! That's it."

Stacy *urrmp*ed.

Granny nodded. "Good point. Stacy says animals also enjoy their sleep."

"Whoa! Granny!" I exclaimed. "Do you talk *steg*?"

Granny rolled her eyes. "Oona, of course I speak a basic dinosaur dialect! My parents, your great-grandthunks, were from dinosaur times! And speaking of times, it's time for my morning nap. Wake me up when things get interesting." Then she climbed a nearby yucca tree.

Soon we could hear Granny's snores drifting down.

Bruce Brute was first to arrive with Baa.

"Good morning!" I called out. "Welcome to drop-off! But what's wrong, Bruce?" He looked a little down.

"Granny Grandthunk challenged me to a sunrise push-up contest this morning," answered Bruce. "Winner had to hand over his shoes. Now my bare feet are sore from walking."

"Sorry about that, Bruce. But you better watch out for Granny," I warned. "She looks as sweet as a fruitafossor, but she's really as fierce as a saber-toothed tiger."

Bruce nodded. "My feet wish they'd known that earlier." He passed Bonk his goat's leash. "Here's my pet. Ready for camp."

"Name of camper?" I asked. I knew Baa's name but I wanted to sound official.

"Baa Brute."

"Male or female?" I knew that, too.

"Male." Bruce hugged Baa. "Bye-bye, Baa."

In answer, Baa *baa*ed, and then stuck his tongue up his own nose. Bruce grinned. "Smart boy! I taught him that! See you at sundown!"

By now, other kids had arrived, filing behind Bruce with their own animals. One by one, they dropped off their pets and said their good-byes.

Bonk handled the shell- or scale-covered animals, because he was allergic to fur. Granny handled the furry ones. I checked off the names.

Soon we had a long list of campers!

What a variety! As the pets were checked in, they formed a ring around the snack piles. Soon they were chewing contentedly. "This should be a camp tradition," I said. "Let's call it Circle Time."

LIST OF CAMP WOGGLE PETS

Storm E. Gurd—
fruitafossor

Rain E. Gurd—
fruitafossor

Vernon Rode—snake

Snert & Sandy Droog, plus their kids, Snert Jr., Iz, and

Nancy Droog—
lizards

Stacy Steg
Oodlethunk—
stegosaurus

Ganu Brouhaha
—sloth

Baa Brute—goat

Keanu
McGuck—turtle

Min Urmson—lemur

Keith Stalagmite
—rock

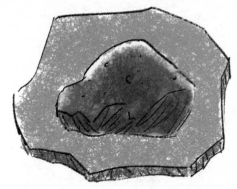

"And best of all," said Bonk, "you-know-who didn't show."

"Yep, and I'm glad," I said. "Camp is not the right place for a—"

I didn't even get to finish the sentence before monkeys and birds started chattering in the trees. "Egad!" I tried out Dad's word. I knew what that noise meant!

From around a thatch of young bristlecone trees, who should appear but—

Mauro and Inglebert!

The first thing I noticed was that Bonk and I had been right.

By the light of day, anyone could see that Inglebert was only a baby T. rex.

By the light of day, anyone could also see that this baby T. rex was a cutie-patootie. That

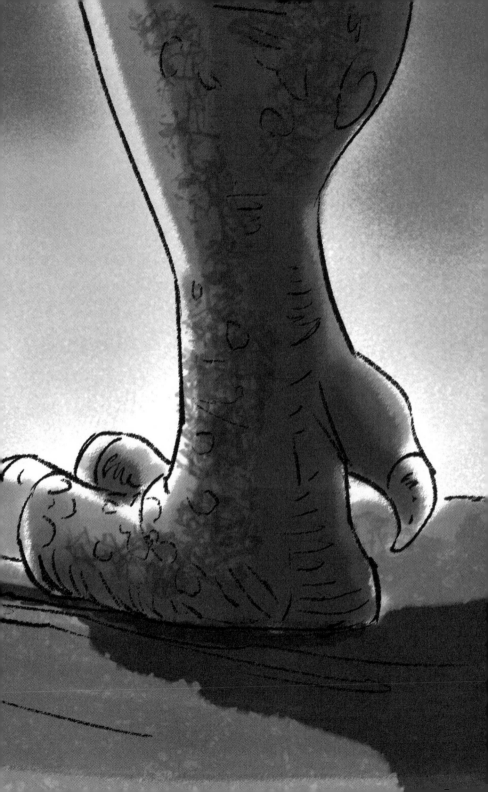

oversized wobbly head! Those teeny hands! That big toothy grin!

(On second thought, the big toothy grin was completely terrifying.)

"Oona and Bonk, please let me introduce you to Inglebert. He wants to join your camp. He promises he will be on his best behavior." It sounded like Mauro had been practicing this speech.

"Inglebert is a dangerous predator. He is a total violation of Camp Woggle rule number four. Maybe you should find a deadly predator camp for him." I had been practicing my speech, too. Just in case.

"Inglebert is only a predator when he needs to eat," Mauro protested. "Before we got here, I fed him a dozen scrambled duck eggs. Ing won't be hungry again until dinner. He is so totally harmless." Mauro turned to his pet. "Come on, Ing. Show everyone how cute and fun you are."

Inglebert sprang up, jumped, and hung upside down from the branch of a bristlecone tree by

his little T. rex tail. Then he bounced to his feet and showed us some intimidation tactics—but as soon as I got too scared, he rolled over and played dead.

"That was cute and fun," admitted Bonk.

"Now watch this." Mauro took a bone from his pocket and threw it out of sight. "Ing, fetch."

Inglebert dashed off. He returned with the bone in his teeth.

"Ing, drop," said Mauro.

Inglebert shook his head.

"Drop!" said Mauro.

Inglebert chomped down the bone in a single crunch.

Mauro turned to me. "We're working on that. Still, as you can see, nothing about Inglebert is dangerous."

Stacy had crept up behind me to watch Inglebert. I could feel her frightened breath on the back of my neck.

"I'm sorry, Mauro. I have a bad feeling about this," I said. "I command Inglebert to go."

Mauro looked sad. Then he set his face to: STUBBORN.

Reluctantly, I raised my club. I set my face to: STUBBORN WARNING.

In the way back of his throat, Inglebert growled.

In the way back of her throat, Stacy growled back.

Alerted, the other animals stopped snacking.

"Ah! Looks like things are getting interesting around here!" With a thump, Granny had unrolled from the tree to land on her feet. "Whaddaya know! A real live T. rex! What's his name?"

"Inglebert," said Mauro.

"Welcome to camp, Inglebert!"

"He's not welcome," I said.

"Why not?" asked Granny.

"Because this isn't a dangerous predator camp," said Bonk.

Granny reached out and gave Inglebert a rub on the nose. "If you want your animals to have fun at Camp Woggle, you need team leaders with team spirit. Everyone knows T. rexes are *very* spirited."

"He's also a good protector. And he sleeps on the foot of my bed slab," said Mauro. "That's how much I trust him."

I glanced over at our other campers.

Maybe we did need to get some camp spirit into the mix.

I looked back at Inglebert. He sat back on his hind legs and made a funny face, trying to look harmless. Which I knew he wasn't.

Camp Woggle was waiting for my decision.

"We have some conditions," I said. "First, Mauro, you should stick around camp for a while. You need to supervise Inglebert while he adjusts to his new habitat."

Mauro nodded.

"Second," I said, "if Inglebert is a team leader, Stacy should be a team leader, too—in the spirit of healthy camp competition."

"Yes." Bonk nodded. "But no real fighting. Just play fighting."

"Exactly," said Granny. "So if Inglebert eats a camper—and let's face it, there's a good chance that he will—he's got to go."

"Got it," said Mauro. He turned to Inglebert. "Got it?"

Inglebert made a peaceful snorting sound. Mauro looked at us. "He gets it."

Wow. Mauro spoke a dino dialect, too? That seemed even cooler to me than knowing the word *habitat*.

"It's settled, then." We clonked our clubs in agreement.

"Campers, meet our newest addition, Inglebert," I announced.

The pets all looked petrified.

"He isn't dangerous," I said.

The pets did not look convinced.

"Stacy and Inglebert are also the coheads of Camp Woggle's teams, the Stegomazings and Rextastics!" added Bonk.

Good names, Bonk! I gave him a thumbs-up.

"So let's count off teams," I said, "and get to know your team leader, pets—because the Camp Woggle fun starts NOW!"

STEGOMAZINGS

REXTASTICS

CAMPER DOWN, CAMPER DOWN!

Inglebert was smart. Very smart.

He was smarter than a ferret or a lizard, or even a fruitafossor.

He was way smarter than a goat.

And as hard as it was for Bonk and me to admit, young Inglebert was even smarter than our darling Stacy Steg Oodlethunk.

On his first day as a West Woggle camper, Inglebert had figured out everything we needed to create a perfect camp atmosphere. For example, he invented:

Camp Woggle's camp game: wag-tag!

Camp Woggle's camp battle cry: ROAAAHHHR!

d hand-eye coordination and track-
uprooting.

had other, unexpected skills, like the
wed off at Crafts Time. His nimble
ld hold a brush as well as any profes-
-wall painter. The other pets had to
rushes in their mouths, but mostly
do any crafts. They just waited for us
afts for them.

imes I feel sorry for Stacy," said Bonk
back in our cave, after Stacy was
e whole family was sitting around the
ab, enjoying Granny's favorite dish:
soup.

?" asked Mom.

use Inglebert is such a star at Camp
He can do anything!"

y wins the heavy-lifting and basic
categories," I said.

y is also the best leg-wrestler," said
slurping a slug. "I'll need to practice
ay to beat her."

Camp Woggle's camp song: "Hoo-ahh! Hoo-ahhh hoo-ahhh GRRRR! Hoo-ahh! Hoo-ahhh hoo-ahhh GRRRR! Hoo-ahh! Hoo-ahhh hoo-ahhh GRRRR!"

(Repeat seven more times.)

Inglebert was also our fastest runner, our highest jumper, and our official camp jokester.

At sundown, when kids came to pick up their pets, we had to inform every pet owner that Inglebert was now enrolled at Camp Woggle.

"Ehhhhhhhhh," said Meadow.

"Errrrrrrrrr," said Erma.

"Uuuurrrrrr," said Bruce.

Kids could not hide their fear. Everyone remembered Inglebert from the potluck. Nobody was too thrilled that he was here.

But the next day, the only camper who didn't return to Camp Woggle was our lemur, Min Urmson.

Urm Urmson came by Old Tooth Fort himself to let us know. "I'm sure that Min would have loved camp, if she'd been awake for it," he said. "But Min is nocturnal."

"Min slept through Circle Time and she slept through Morning Exercises and she slept through Games and she slept through Crafts.

She was reall[y] acknowledged. woke up."

Urm looked ov[er] between his paws. could see every on[e] and crunching tee[th] be asleep all day [at] Woggle," said Urm[son]

"I agree, Urm," guard."

So was Granny. S[he] But after a few da[ys] fact, Mauro didn't e[ven] anymore.

Why not?

Because Inglebert w[as]

strength an[d] ing and tre[e] But Ing[lebert] ones he sh[ould] fingers cou[ld] sional cave[?] hold the [?] pets didn't[?] to make c[?]

"Some[?] one nigh[t] asleep. Th[?] dinner sh[?] slug-neck[?]

"Why[?] "Beca[use] Woggle. "Stac[?] strength[?] "Stac[?] Granny[?] every d[ay]

"Stacy is mostly just happy being Stacy," I said. "She knows how awesome she is."

"It doesn't matter who is king at Camp Woggle, as long as camp is a kind and thoughtful place," said Dad. "Is it?"

"I think so! Everyone loves it," I said. "And we tire out the pets, too. Listen to how hard Stacy is snoring in the yard! She's louder than Granny!"

"Who are you calling a snorer?" barked Granny.

"I don't know how you handle that terrifying, full-grown T. rex all day." Mom scratched her head with her knuckles.

"I'm surprised he hasn't eaten Granny by now," added Dad.

Bonk and I exchanged a secret smile. We had decided Mom and Dad would have felt too embarrassed to know that they'd run away from a little baby T. rex.

So we never told them.

"It's getting pretty hot on Slabtop's

mountainside," I said, to change the subject. "Tomorrow we're taking the campers down to No-Name River. It will be our first camp field trip."

"Fun! Do all your pets swim?" asked Mom.

"Yes! Every one of them can swim except for Keith Stalagmite," said Bonk.

"But since Keith is a rock, it's not really a problem," I added.

As it turned out, I was wrong about that.

The next morning, the Camp Woggle field trip started perfectly. We made each pet hold a notch of one long vine by his or her mouth so that we could proceed single file down Slabtop Mountain and then over to No-Name River, which ran between Slabtop and Mount Urp.

When we got to the river, Inglebert invented a game for the Rextastics versus the

Stegomazings, where the pets jumped off a low ledge and raced out to a big flat rock in the middle of the water.

Soon the pets were diving and splashing. In fact, there was so much splashing that I decided to watch from a safe, dry place on Clodhopper Bridge. I sat and swung my legs off the side. From where I was, the campers seemed to be having a great time! It warmed my heart to see them.

SMASH! In dove Inglebert. It was a perfect dive that barely rippled the surface.

Splish! In jumped Storm and Rain.

Smash! In dropped Baa, kicking up his heels.

Blop! In dropped Keanu, right to the top of his turtle shell.

Plip plip plip plip plip . . . in slithered the Droog family lizards.

KER-PLASH! For giant Stacy, the river was more like a big wading pool.

Granny was swimming around out by the rock, making sure all the pets were pulled in to safety. After a while, she started waving at me.

I waved back.

Granny waved harder. She was saying something.

"What?" My left ear twitched to hear.

"Camper down! Camper down!"

Camper down? Oh no! I stood up and *splash!* I jumped off the bridge and swam out to the rock. There, the pets were in a state of panic, shaking and chattering and pointing.

But Inglebert wasn't chattering or pointing.

He was looking very sad. So were Bonk and Granny.

"What happened?!" I asked.

"I hate to say I told you so," said Granny. "But Inglebert ate a camper."

"Which one?" I gasped.

"Keith."

"Oh no!" My knees buckled. "Keith is Meadow's beloved pet rock! How did he even get out here?"

"I took him," said Bonk. "I didn't want to leave him alone on the riverbank. I thought he'd be safe on my watch." He looked at Inglebert. "Guess I was wrong."

Inglebert hung his head. He made a few small, unhappy noises.

"Ing says he had low blood sugar," said Granny. "He didn't get enough snack during Circle Time."

It was true the snacks were a bit lean this morning. Running a camp, there was always so much to do! We had to gather snacks on the fly, and sometimes there weren't enough to go around. But it was still hard to look Meadow Stalagmite in the eye at sundown pickup, when I had to tell her someone had eaten her pet.

"WHO? Who did it?!" Meadow wailed.

"Per our Camp Woggle policy, we are protecting the offender's name," I said.

Meadow's eyes narrowed. "Was it Stacy? Everyone knows that stegs love to eat rocks!"

"Of course it wasn't Stacy!" I snapped.

"I trusted Camp Woggle to keep Keith safe! Now I'll never kiss his little painted rock face again!" Meadow wailed. "I'll never rub his smooth rock belly! I'll never watch another sundown while holding his warm little rock self in my hand! There will never be another rock like my sweet Keith!"

She took up her club and pounded it in the ground.

"I'm sorry, Meadow," I told her. "I understand how you feel. It wasn't so long ago that my steg was an egg. People always told me it was a fossil or a rock. But it actually didn't matter to me. Egg, rock, fossil—I loved it."

But Meadow just wiped her eyes and dragged off in despair, trailing her club behind her.

She was too sad for my words to help.

When Mauro came to pick up Inglebert, I gave him the bad news.

"I'm so disappointed in you, Ing," said Mauro. "We should go apologize to Meadow right now." He turned to Bonk and me. "What's the penalty?"

"I think we should put Ing on probation," I said.

"I agree. We don't have to kick him out, since Keith Stalagmite was not an *alive* camper," said Bonk. "I think an alive camper would be much worse."

"Exactly," I said. "Ing gets to stay at Camp Woggle—for now."

"But this can't happen again," said Granny. "It's just not good camp spirit."

"We promise that it won't," said Mauro. "Right, Ing?"

Ing nodded. He and Mauro did both look very sorry.

But I'd seen Inglebert look sorry one minute and ferocious the next.

How could Mauro guarantee what Ing might do?

As I watched them both leave, I realized that, for the very first time, I was a little bit petrified to have a T. rex at Camp Woggle.

STRIKE TWO

For a nice long stretch, the sunny days at Camp Woggle passed smoothly. Inglebert was always on his best behavior. When the snacks were lean and he got hungry, Ing learned how to fill up on water and weeds.

He also taught Stacy how to push against Slabtop's chokecherry trees until the smaller branches snapped and fell to the ground.

Then Ing and Stace split the flavorful twigs and cherries between them.

Stacy gobbled down half and burped with joy.

Inglebert chewed on a few twigs. He was not a natural vegetarian.

"I'm glad Inglebert is trying to expand his

carnivore diet," said Granny. "He is taking that new rule number six, No Eating Live Campers, very seriously."

"And it's great to see these pets learning how to get along," said Bonk.

"All in all, Camp Woggle has been a cool idea," I said. "It's too bad that pet owners can't see the progress our campers have made this summer."

"But what if they could?" said Bonk.

"Like, what if we had a special day for kids to come see?" I asked.

"Yes. Like a Field Day," said Granny.

"Great name, Granny!" Bonk and I high-fived.

"With leg-wrestling!" said Granny.

We went silent on that one.

To practice events for Field Day, we often relocated Camp Woggle to the cool, muddy banks of No-Name River. There, Inglebert and Stacy, as team captains, guided the pets on honing their skills.

Ing was a natural coach. Even though he was the youngest camper, he was a smart teacher of racing, jumping, and charging.

And Stacy had the most camp spirit. She was ever ready to lend her strength, or *urrrrmp* her encouragement, or offer a ride to a tired camper.

"We really lucked out on these two charming dinosaurs," said Granny. "It's a pity that they are mostly extinct."

When Camp Woggle wasn't training for Field Day, we led the campers on exploring trips. We collected leaves and cattails and rocks (none were as good-looking as Keith). In the afternoon, the shade was always comfortable, with the sun dappling through the canopy of firs and bristlecone branches.

Our riverbank location had only one problem: Our campsite was next to a hollow log, where a family of porcupines lived.

The porcupines didn't like Camp Woggle being so close.

"I don't blame them," said Bonk. "We can get pretty rowdy."

"It's true. And yesterday Stacy almost stood on a baby porcupine," I said. "But when you're as big as Stace, a porcupine probably looks the same size as a bristlecone."

"At least we're not boiling hot like we were up on Slabtop," said Granny. "I'll leg-wrestle any porcupine who tries to make us leave."

The silver-quilled Grandpa Porcupine seemed especially angry about our campers. Every morning, as soon as he heard us, he would stomp out to the top of the log and pound his feet and point and chatter.

"Good thing nobody speaks porcupine," I said with a shudder. But I wanted to keep the peace, and so one morning I gathered treats for the porcupines: sour berries and a few long, curled shavings of birch bark.

The porcupines happily snarfed my treats— but Grandpa didn't get any nicer.

"Ignore him," said Granny and Bonk.

"I think you're wrong," I said. "I think we've got a problem."

"Two against one," said Granny and Bonk.

I tried to ignore Grandpa Porcupine. I refocused. With Field Day just around the corner, the pet excitement was in a full tilt.

One day on the riverbank, Granny and I left Bonk in charge of the campers so that we could prepare lunch. We always made our camp lunches special. Today Granny prepared a few dozen tasty leaf-wrapped summer slugs. I skinned a batch of sour plums. I filled the water bowls, and lastly, I swept a clean patch of ground so that we could eat together, picnic-style.

Then we heard it. Shouting, squeaking, growling, barking—what was going on?

"Oh no!" Granny and I grabbed our clubs and looked at each other.

Noise like that meant one thing!

"ING!" we hollered at the same time.

We sprinted to the riverbank.

It was porcupine mayhem! All our campers were making a commotion, while the whole porc family had clambered out of the log to hiss and squeak at Inglebert.

At the center of the storm, the T. rex was being very quiet. He was holding his claws over

his stomach and spitting out silver quills by the dozen.

"What's happening here?" I shouted.

"More importantly WHAT OR WHO DID ING EAT?" cried Granny.

"He ate Grandpa Porcupine," Bonk answered. "I saw it myself. He went down quick."

Inglebert grunted deep in his throat.

Granny's eyes got wide. "Ing thinks he's helped us out. He says he took care of a problem."

"Ing!" I stamped my feet. "This has got to stop! When you eat other creatures, your behavior is too savage for Camp Woggle!"

I shook my club at him.

But the porcupines thought my club shake meant I planned to attack Ing. With their teeth bared and their spines spiked, they rushed the baby T. rex.

Ing was not one bit scared of a prickle of porcupines. As soon as he saw them coming, he opened his enormous mouth and ROAAAAAAAARED!

That did it.

Every porcupine jumped headlong back into the log.

And the log went dead silent.

When Mauro picked up Ing at the end of the day, he was sad to get the news.

"The only reason Ing can stay at Camp Woggle is because porcupines aren't campers," said Granny. "Which means, technically, that they are snacks. Don't forget, West Woggle's motto is 'Eat or be Eaten.'"

"Also, Grandpa Porcupine wasn't anyone's pet," said Bonk.

"Now just hang on a second," I said. "I know we love Ing. But he needs to learn! Even if Grandpa Porcupine was a grouch. Even if Grandpa wasn't a

camper. Even if Grandpa wasn't a pet. Grandpa Porcupine was still someone's grandpa."

"We will go apologize to the porcupines right now," said Mauro. "But I have a question. Can Inglebert please compete at Field Day tomorrow? It's all he ever grunts about at home."

"Ugh. I don't know." I frowned.

Ing rolled over on his back to show his soft underbelly. He batted his long brown eyelashes.

"Our Field Day wouldn't be half as fun without Inglebert," said Bonk.

I went over to Inglebert and put one hand on either side of his huge head. I stared into his big brown eyes.

"Ing, do you think you can promise you will not swallow one more precious creature while you are at Camp Woggle?"

Ing grunted.

Granny and Mauro nodded. "He promises," they said.

"Okay," I said. "You are invited to Field Day. But don't forget—this is strike two. You ate

Keith Stalagmite. You ate Grandpa Porcupine. Three strikes and you're out of Camp Woggle for good."

"Got it?" asked Bonk.

Ing held up three fingers and nodded.

Got it.

No matter what else you might want to say about him, Inglebert Ongeri was one smart little T. rex.

SO, SO, SO, SO, SO CLOSE

Field Day dawned hot. Bonk and I knew it would be a scorcher, because we were up with the sun.

In the front yard, Stacy and Granny were already awake. They were sharing one last leg-wrestling practice.

"Granny's getting good," I said.

"True. But Stacy is at least thirty times bigger than Granny," said Bonk.

As we searched for morning snacks to take up to Slabtop, Bruce Brute came out of his cave and did something he'd never done before.

He helped.

"Big day today!" said Bruce as he gathered

up a pile of thistles. "Baa is really looking forward to it!"

"Us too," said Bonk. "See ya there!"

"If Bruce is helping out with Field Day, then I would say Camp Woggle is a hit," I announced proudly as Stacy, Granny, Bonk, and I trudged from Mount Urp over to Slabtop.

"No doubt about it!" said Granny. "I've changed my mind about camp. These pets have improved. Nobody likes a lazy pet! But a pet with real skills? One that can fetch and do tricks and competes in a pet relay? Now that pet's a keeper!"

As we went on our way, everyone who saw us walking along our path called out.

"See you soon, Oodlethunks!"

"Can't wait for Field Day!"

"We're excited to see what these pets can do!"

At Old Tooth Fort, campers checked in early. They were hopping with excitement. They knew that today was the day they'd be able to show everyone what they could do.

All morning, they devoted themselves to practice.

Ganu Brouhaha practiced his best upside-down hanging.

Vernon Rode performed his slithery snake dancing.

Storm and Rain Gurd worked on their termite act.

Baa Brute got in a few final back-kicking high jumps.

And the Droog lizards jumped from leaf to leaf, changing colors.

Meantime, Bonk, Granny, and I used the whole morning to set up. First we created the obstacle course for the Pet Relay. Then we cleared a large stage around the riverbank for Skills and Talents. And then we assembled the seat slabs so that everyone could watch.

"Kids are gonna be so proud of their pets," said Bonk.

"Us most of all," I said. "I will be proud of every single pet in our whole pet camp family!"

To sprinkle some extra specialness onto Field Day, Dad had made us some of his Oodlethunk Delights: his apple stew, along with a large stack of buckwheat-acorn roll-ups. I also arranged the pet treats: yucca, hay, and moss.

Everything looked perfect. At midday, we saw the first Wogglers beginning to trickle over the bridge from Mount Urp.

"I'm glad we are having some of Field Day close to the water," I mentioned.

"No joke!" Granny had already taken a morning river dunk. "Looks like another boiling hot day on Slabtop. Be prepared!"

Soon pets and watchers had assembled into place. People were wiping their brows and passing the water buckets. Otherwise the crowds were ready!

Bonk and I went to the middle of the clearing to deliver our speech.

"THANK YOU FOR COMING TO OUR FANTASTIC FIELD DAY!" I shouted.

upside-down

High Jumps!

Snake Dance!

Termite Show!

CAMOUflage

"WE HOPE YOU ENJOY WATCHING YOUR PETS!" bellowed Bonk.

That was the end of our speech.

Everyone clapped their hands and stomped their feet.

Field Day was about to start.

"First up is leg wrestling," announced Bonk. "Our very own Stacy Oodlethunk takes on our also very own Granny Grandthunk!"

Granny sprang to the middle of the clearing. "I've been working on my leg wrestling all summer," she said. "This should be a really thrilling match, folks!" She rubbed her hands together. "Best outta three!"

It turned out to be more like a really quick match.

"Uncle!" Granny yelped.

"Uncle!" Granny croaked.

"Uncle!" Granny whimpered.

"Granny got pinned three times in under a minute," I exclaimed.

"Stacy Steg Oodlethunk continues her

unbroken reign as leg-wrestling champion of West Woggle!" yelled Bonk.

The crowd hooted and whistled. Stacy was the popular choice for sure.

"Attagirl, Stace!" Dad was cheering the loudest of anyone.

Granny bounced up, dusting herself off. "Stacy was easier on me during practice! Not to worry, I will keep practicing! Until next summer!" She went and sat on the sidelines in a determined huff.

Next up were Storm and Rain.

"Behold the termite jugglers!" I declared. The two fruitafossors counted off a few paces, then spun around and faced each other.

Rain served the termite first, tapping it high and aloft.

Pop pop pop pop! The termite bounced effortlessly between the fruitafossors. From nose to nose and back again.

The crowed oohed and aahed.

Termite bouncing—when done well—is truly spectacular to watch!

"I counted fifty bounces. Not once was that termite dropped!" hollered Erma Gurd. "It's got to be a record!"

"We are proud pet owners today!" said Iggy Gurd.

The fruitafossors also looked proud. But the termite mostly looked dizzy, so it must have been a relief when Storm ate him.

"And now Baa Brute, West Woggle's most graceful goat, will show off his jumping skills," announced Bonk.

Baa cleared every single hurdle we'd set up with surprising grace and beauty. (Especially considering that he belonged to Bruce Brute.)

"Ooooh!" Wogglers pounded the ground in appreciation.

Bruce beamed.

"And for our next talent," I announced, with lots of dramatic flavor, "we have something more refined to offer. Inglebert Ongeri will paint a landscape on this slab of stone!"

Bonk had already set the paint slab and pots of paint against a boulder. Everyone went quiet. Wogglers craned in for a look.

Inglebert appeared from behind a rock. Everyone tried not to gasp in fear.

With flair, he took up his brush. Quickly, he jabbed bright splodges of red and blue and green paint across his slab. An abstract landscape began to form.

Wogglers were flabbergasted. A murmur rose up in the crowd.

"What artistic fingers!"

"What daring composition!"

"What fine technical style!"

"His sense of color is so modern!"

"Eh. I'm not a fan of modern art," whispered Old Brouhaha. "If you're going to paint a woolly mammoth, I want to see four legs and two tusks."

"You're just an old-school savage, Old Brou." Granny tsked.

Mauro was pleased that everyone saw Inglebert for what he was: a star. "Ing thinks of himself as an artist first," said Mauro. "This praise means a lot to him."

The last, best event of Field Day was the Pet Relay.

We all had planned hardest for this one.

This was where our campers showed off their skills in speed, teamwork, and coordination. We knew the rules because we played a version of Pet Relay at school, but we didn't call it Pet Relay. We just called it Relay.

Just like school, the campers were divided into two teams—the Rextastics against Stegomazings.

Just like school, everyone was included, from the slowest to the fastest runners.

Unlike school, the stick that the Camp Wogglers passed was a twig. So even our smallest campers could balance it in their mouths.

Bonk, Granny, and I had created the relay so that it wound from upper Slabtop all the way down to the valley finish line. We placed a crock of black-bean brownies next to the finish. Win or lose, everyone enjoyed Dad's black-bean brownies. Even though Dad had invented them as an Oodlethunk Delight for people, it turned out that animals liked them, too.

"LAST EVENT OF FIELD DAY IS PET RELAY!" I shouted.

The pets got into position.

The thrill of sports competition put an extra zing in the air.

"AND THEY'RE OFF!" yelled Bonk. "BANG!" he added, for emphasis.

Ganu and Keanu were slow. Sloth slow. Turtle slow.

So slow that, while it was their turn, we got snacks or took short naps.

But finally, the pass-off! Ganu passed his twig to Stacy, while Keanu nudged his twig over to Baa.

All eyes were on Stacy and Baa! The steg and the goat came crashing through the West Woggle underbrush. This Pet Relay was too close to call!

But it looked like Stacy was a tiny bit ahead as she and Baa passed off their twigs to Storm and Rain.

"Storm and Rain have narrowed the margin again! It's too hard to say who'll win!" reported Thodunk Rode, who was watching from high up in a bristlecone tree. "Storm just did a twig pass to my very own sports snake, Vernon. That speedy Rain has passed to Ezra Droog's lizard, Nancy!"

Around a horsetail plant came Team Rextastic's Vernon Rode!

Around a thicket, in a burst of speed, came Team Stegomazings's Nancy Droog!

Quickly it became obvious that Nancy's lizard feet were quicker than Vernon's slither.

Still, the creatures were just about snake neck–to–lizard neck when—

From the sidelines, a nimble hand shot out.

And Nancy Droog was gone.

The crowd let out a cry of horror.

Uh-oh. I pressed my hands to my mouth. My heart reeled.

"Ugh, ugh, ugh!" said Bonk. "Did you see what happened, Oona?"

"I saw it. But I don't believe it."

On the sidelines, Ezra Droog hollered "Nooooo!" And then he said the thing I had hoped I hadn't seen with my own eyes. Although I knew I had.

"Inglebert ate Nancy Droog!"

"Pet Relay is halted!" called Granny. "A violation has occurred."

Indeed, it had. Nancy Droog was gone.

Emotions were everywhere. But now was not the time to be wimpy.

"INGLEBERT ONGERI!" I used my best bellow. "DID YOU EAT NANCY DROOG

SO THAT THE REXTASTICS COULD WIN PET RELAY?"

Inglebert was standing very still on the sidelines. He shook his head. He tried to say something but his mouth was full.

Then he spit out a twig.

It was the chokecherry twig from the relay.

Last time we'd seen it, Nancy Droog had been carrying it.

I could feel the full force of my feelings gather in the pit of my stomach.

"INGLEBERT!" I shouted. "STRIKE THREE! YOU'RE OUT!"

RUN FOR YOUR LIVES!

Our Field Day broke up pretty quick after that.

Most everyone left in gloom and sadness.

"See you at sundown," I said, waving weakly. But I knew this was a terrible end.

Camp Woggle was a bust. And at the core of the bust was Inglebert, who had broken his promise.

We all had a lot to say about that.

First, Bonk had to bellow at him. Then Granny had to scold him. Then Mauro had to roar at him. Then the Droog lizards had to stick out their tongues.

We were so mad at Inglebert that we weren't watching.

We weren't listening.

We weren't even smelling.

And we really hadn't noticed how boiling, scorching, sizzling hot it was getting. Otherwise maybe we would have known what was happening.

But instead we were too shocked, too angry, and so disappointed in Ing. And by the time everyone was finished being really mad at him

for eating poor defenseless little Nancy Droog, there was almost no time left.

It was Granny who looked up first. "ARGH! Oodlethunks, we gotta move!"

"Move what? Move where? Mom, what are you talking about?" asked Mom.

Just then Thodunk's dad, Nmnk, who was a professional volcano watcher, came tearing through the bramble. His face was red and wild.

"I've waited my whole entire life to say this!" cried Nmnk. "And now I finally can! West Wogglers, this is your volcano warning! Run for your lives! SLABTOP'S GONNA BLOW!!!!!"

"Move NOW!" yelled Granny. She hopped on Stacy. "RUN!"

Nmnk was right! Granny was right! The ground was shaking! Smoke was thickly lifting from up-up-up the granite summit of Slabtop Mountain.

"So *that's* why it's been so hot," said Bonk.

"Kids, we aren't safe!" yelled Mom and Dad,

following Granny's lead and leaping onto Stacy. "Save yourselves!"

"But what do we do about the pets?" Bonk was thinking my own thoughts out loud. "They have no survival skills! They've been raised as objects of love!"

"With limited instincts!" My pulse was pounding. The pets seemed to have gone into pure shock.

"You heard Nmnk!" By now Mom and Dad had pulled us onto Stacy. Desperately I looked around—and then my gaze fell on you-know-who.

My idea was out there. A little bit nuts. But it just might work.

I ran to Inglebert and put a hand on each side of his enormous face. I stared into his warm brown eyes.

"Inglebert, I know in my heart how much you love Camp Woggle," I told him. "But if you really want to make up for today, you'll need to do something pretty crazy."

Inglebert looked at me worriedly. Listening.

"You will need to let every small defenseless pet in Camp Woggle ride on your head and shoulders as you run them to safety. You might even need to stick a few littler pets in your mouth. AND YOU CANNOT EAT ANY OF THEM!"

Ing shook his head like he'd never do such a thing. He made a few short grunts.

"He gets it," said Mauro, wiping his sweaty brow. "But we better go NOW."

"These are your teammates!" I told Ing. "These are your fellow campers! And most importantly, these are your friends!"

Ing *rmph*ed. Ing pawed the earth with his huge feet. Then he opened his ENORMOUS mouth, as an invitation.

"Get on Ing!" I ordered the pets. "It's your only chance. If you aren't strong enough to hold on to his back, you can hold on to his teeth. He promises you will not be his next meal!"

"Take a chance, pets!" roared Granny.

"Because you don't have a choice! Molten hot lava is flowing our way!"

The pets jumped on Ing. The lizards' weren't strong enough to do anything but dive inside Ing's mouth. With all those teeth, it was a scary risk.

Then we tore our way down Slabtop Mountain. We didn't stop until we had gotten across the water and over to Mount Urp.

Safe on the other side, we looked up and watched the magnificent volcano erupt in a spew of lava. The noise was deafening! It was bursting, bubbling, hissing, and roaring! There were booms and blasts of gasses as pressure from the mountain's core blew its top!

The ground shook beneath our feet. We coughed away the thick, billowing clouds of smoke.

"That's it for Old Tooth Fort, I guess," said Bonk.

"Yes, Old Tooth Fort is toast," said Nmnk, who was coming around with his tablet taking

a head count. "All the citizens of Woggle are here!" he announced happily. But then he looked sad. "I don't think the pets got away."

There was a noise. We looked up. High on a ledge, safe from the volcanic ash, stood Inglebert, with every single pet on Camp Woggle clinging to him.

Mauro joined Ing's side to help the pets dismount.

"The whole porcupine family rode on Ing," exclaimed Bonk. "I hadn't even seen them jump on!"

"And the lizards are jumping out of Ing's mouth, safe and sound."

One of the lizards that leaped down looked familiar.

Was that . . . ? I stepped closer. It was!

Nancy Droog scuttled to the edge of the ledge and stretched her webbed feet.

"Nancy! I thought you were a goner!"

Ing made some grunt noises. Mauro nodded,

listening. When he turned to speak to us, his smile was broad.

"Ing is very sorry that he swiped Nancy so that he could win the relay," said Mauro. "He said he never planned to eat her. She got stuck in his way back fifty-eighth tooth. He couldn't explain himself because he worried that if he used his mouth, he'd bite her. He hopes you will forgive him."

"Ing, you're forgiven," I told him. "In fact, today you are a hero among pets!"

Then we all went back to looking at the erupting volcano.

From a (safe) distance, it looked very beautiful.

AND THE AWARD GOES TO . . .

Slabtop Mountain was no longer a slab. It was more like a blasted hollow dome. Once the eruption died, we Wogglers lay low and just let it smoke.

The end-of-summer rainstorms helped to cool down the mountain big-time.

When it seemed safe enough to explore, Erma and I decided to visit the newly named Dometop Mountain.

"The whole entire side of this mountain has changed," Erma observed.

"Check out these cool volcanic rocks!" I pointed.

"The intense heat made some really

interesting shapes and colors," said Erma. We both used our clubs to poke at them. "Look at this jagged one!"

"And this one looks like a hard ball of twine!" I exclaimed.

"And this one sparkles like a starry night!"

We decided to put the rocks into our basket and take them home to show the others.

"You can never tell when nature will play one of its tricks," I said. "But this volcano sure was a dangerous end to camp."

"It's too bad," said Erma, "because our pets really loved Camp Woggle. And camp should not end with a volcano."

As I gathered rocks to the top of the basket, I thought about what Erma had said. She was right, of course. Camp Woggle should not have ended with a volcano.

And I should be the one to fix that.

Later that night, when we were gathered around the fire, I brought out my entire

Volcanic Rocks

collection of Dometop Mountain rocks for my family to inspect.

"How pretty!" Mom picked out one and held it to the light.

"I was thinking that Bonk and I should give a beautiful rock to each of our campers," I said. "Kind of as a nicer way to remember Camp Woggle than the volcano."

"I like that. The pets and owners could come over to our cave to get them. We could make it a party," said Dad. "Camp Woggle definitely needs closure."

"Honey, what is *closure*?" asked Mom.

"I just invented it," said Dad. "Closure is making time and space for everyone to understand their feelings about Camp Woggle."

"That definitely sounds like one of your inventions, Dave," said Granny.

"Closure also needs prizes," said Bonk. "Who doesn't like a prize?"

We decided that we should give every camper

the same prize—a rock—but that each prize should have a different meaning. So Bonk and I spent the next few days painting individual rocks with each camper's portrait.

Then, party time!

We invited everyone over to our backyard for sundown refreshments and prizes.

We lined up the rocks on Mom's rock wall.

Dad made a giant bowl of apricot smash, along with stinging-nettles salad and his old classic, fried newt fingers. I was glad we did not have any campers who were newts, or they might have been offended.

The Ongeris were the first to arrive. They brought not one but two chickpea pies!

"Oh, YEAH! I want firsts, seconds, and thirds right now!" I hollered.

Ing leaped around and licked Stacy.

"He really missed her," said Mauro. "He missed everyone."

Once the campers and their pets were assembled, Bonk and I stood to make our final speech of the summer.

This time we kept it *really* short.

"TIME FOR PRIZES!" we both shouted.

"We would like to give out a prize to every camper who made Camp Woggle such a special, fun, kind experience," I said. "So please come up and get your rock."

We called out the names of each camper that we had engraved on our rock tablet:

THE PRIZES:

Storm E. Gurd & Rain E. Gurd,
    fruitafossors—best balancers
Vernon Rode—snake, best dancer
Snert & Sandy Droog, Snert Jr., Iz, and
    Nancy Droog—lizards, nicest
    teamwork
Stacy Steg Oodlethunk—stegosaurus,
    most camp spirit
Inglebert Ongeri—T. rex, best coach
Ganu Brouhaha—sloth, most patient
Baa Brute—goat, highest jumper
Keanu McGuck—turtle, best sunbather
Min Urmson—lemur, longest napper
Keith Stalagmite—rock, most missed

Each pet proudly held his or her rock carefully in its teeth.

Meadow accepted Keith's prize on his behalf. "A little rock to remember a big one," she said. "Thank you."

"And finally, we want to give a prize to somebody who has shown us what it means to never give up. The award for the best leg-wrestler who did not once win a single leg-wrestling match goes to . . . Granny Grandthunk!"

Wooo-hooo! Everyone clapped and stomped. Even Dad.

Granny smiled down at her rock portrait. Bonk and I had signed her rock with love from us both. "I was not expecting that," she said. "Ugh, some volcano dust just got in my eye." She wiped it. "Thank you."

"We hope you come back next summer,

Granny," I said honestly. "Camp Woggle wouldn't be the same without you."

"AND NOW, LET'S EAT!" Bonk shouted.

The pets were really glad to play with one another.

In a way, it was just like camp all over again.

At the end of the party, Meadow and her parents, Urf and Linda, came up to Bonk and me.

"We have some news we want to share," said Meadow with a shy smile. "I wanted you all to be the first to see." She opened a small clay pot.

Bonk and I looked. Inside the pot was a large leaf.

On the leaf was a big, fat, juicy green garden slug.

"Meet my new pet, Baily," said Meadow proudly. "He is also my first live pet. Baily, meet Oona and Bonk!"

"Awwwww," said Bonk.

"Meadow, he's adorable!" I told her.

"After I lost Keith," said Meadow, "I realized how much I wanted to love something again."

She drew herself up to her full, responsible height. "But now I'm ready for an alive thing."

"You couldn't have picked a more delicious-looking little guy," said Granny.

The slug stared blindly up at us.

"Baily loves naps, clay pots, and resting on leaves," said Meadow. "He has lots of personality. I hope next year he can come to Camp Woggle!"

"Sounds like a plan!" I agreed.

Ing's stomach rumbled loudly.

Granny wiped some drool from the edge of her mouth.

Next year, I would have to remind them *both* about our No Eating Live Campers rule.

Meantime, everywhere I looked I saw good friends, cool pets, and all the chickpea pie that I could eat.

"Woooooo-hoooooooooooo!" I yelled. "Summer!"

AUTHOR'S NOTE:
VOLCANOS OF COLORADO

When we think of Colorado, we do not think of active volcanos. In fact, you would have needed to be alive 4,000 years ago if you wanted to see Colorado's last volcano blow. This happened near the small town of Dotsero, and the Dotsero Crater, at 700 meters in diameter and 76 meters deep, is our only evidence of this massive eruption.

Between thirty and forty million years ago, Colorado enjoyed plenty of volcanic action, which in turn produced its world famous geologic site, the San Juan volcanic field. San Juan's many solidified tuffs (rocks created by volcanic ash) are thought to represent some of the largest eruptions in all of Earth's history. In fact, volcanologists believe that San Juan's volcanic region ejected nearly 5,000 times the amount of material produced by Mount St. Helens.

In real life, a prehistoric volcano probably would have destroyed every single form of life on Slabtop Mountain. But that is a much scarier story than I wanted to tell about the Oodlethunks.

Today, creating an active volcano using baking soda and vinegar is considered to be a perfectly harmless science project.

ABOUT THE AUTHOR

Adele Griffin is the highly acclaimed author of numerous books for middle grade readers, including the Agnes and Clarabelle books with coauthor Courtney Sheinmel. She lives in Brooklyn, New York, with her husband, two children, and their brave eleven-pound dog, Edith. Read more about Bonk and Oona in *Oona Finds an Egg* and *Steg-O-Normous*, the first two books of the Oodlethunks series.

ABOUT THE ARTIST

Mike Wu is the author/illustrator of the critically acclaimed picture book *Ellie*. He is a top animator, working first for Walt Disney and then Pixar, where he animated such Oscar winners as *The Incredibles* and *Toy Story 3* among others, including *Brave*, *Ratatouille*, and *Up*. He is also the cofounder of Tiny Teru, a baby-and-toddler boutique featuring all hand-drawn items. Mike lives in Northern California with his family.

BATS
A group of bats is called a camp — a real-live collective animals meeting place.

SLUG
A slug is a snail-like gastropod with no shell, and a slug-a-bed is someone who likes to sleep.

SLOTH (old Brou's sloth)
Ganu, the sloth in the Oodlethunks, is way too quick for a real sloth. On ground, a sloth can move only about 53 feet per hour.

GOAT
Prehistoric "cave goats" were smaller than today's goats, with forward-facing eyes.

FRUITAFOSSOR
Fruitafossors were prehistoric mammals with powerful forearms, capable of digging for delicious termites.